Dear Parent:
Your child's love of reading starts here!

Every child learns to read in a different way and at his or her own speed. Some go back and forth between reading levels and read favorite books again and again. Others read through each level in order. You can help your young reader improve and become more confident by encouraging his or her own interests and abilities. From books your child reads with you to the first books he or she reads alone, there are I Can Read Books for every stage of reading:

SHARED READING
Basic language, word repetition, and whimsical illustrations, ideal for sharing with your emergent reader

BEGINNING READING
Short sentences, familiar words, and simple concepts for children eager to read on their own

READING WITH HELP
Engaging stories, longer sentences, and language play for developing readers

READING ALONE
Complex plots, challenging vocabulary, and high-interest topics for the independent reader

ADVANCED READING
Short paragraphs, chapters, and exciting themes for the perfect bridge to chapter books

I Can Read Books have introduced children to the joy of reading since 1957. Featuring award-winning authors and illustrators and a fabulous cast of beloved characters, I Can Read Books set the standard for beginning readers.

A lifetime of discovery begins with the magical words **"I Can Read!"**

*Visit www.icanread.com for information
on enriching your child's reading experience.*

Paddington: Paddington's Adventures
Based on the Paddington novels written and created by Michael Bond
PADDINGTON™ and PADDINGTON BEAR™ © Paddington and Company Limited/
STUDIOCANAL S.A. 2014

ISBN 978-0-06-235001-5

14 15 16 17 18 LP/WOR 10 9 8 7 6 5 4 3 2 1
❖
First Edition

PADDINGTON™
Paddington's Adventures

Adapted by Annie Auerbach

Based on the screenplay written by Paul King

Based on the Paddington Bear novels

written and created by Michael Bond

HARPER

An Imprint of HarperCollins*Publishers*

Paddington has had

many adventures.

His first was the journey

from Peru to London.

He stowed away on a ship.

When he arrived in London,

Paddington met the Browns.

The family took him
to find something to eat.
Paddington had never
had tea before!

The Browns took

Paddington home.

He needed to clean himself up.

Paddington had never
been in a bathroom.
When the toilet overflowed,
he climbed out of the way.

To get from his room

to the kitchen,

Paddington slid down

the banister.

The Browns' house

was full of interesting things!

The Browns took Paddington

out one day.

They had to ride

on the Underground.

The Underground sounded exciting,
but Paddington got caught
in the ticket barrier.

Mrs. Brown and Paddington
went to meet Mr. Gruber.

He was an old friend.

They hoped he would be able to help

Paddington find the explorer

who had visited Peru.

At the shop,

Paddington spotted a thief.

He chased the thief

out into the city.

He dodged traffic
and pedestrians.
He even alerted
the police!

Paddington was a hero.
But all of his adventures
were causing trouble
for the Browns.

He decided it was time
to look for the explorer
on his own.

As he searched for the explorer,

he found Millicent.

She offered to help him.

Millicent worked at
the Natural History Museum.
She took Paddington there.

Millicent's office was full
of stuffed animals.
She wanted to add
Paddington to her collection.

Back at the Browns' house,

Mrs. Brown found Paddington's note.

Then they received a call

letting them know where he was.

The Browns raced
to the museum
to rescue Paddington.

Mr. Brown had to climb around the building to reach Paddington in Millicent's office.

Paddington escaped to the roof.

Millicent found him there.

But the Browns

came to rescue him!

Paddington went home

with the Browns.

He'd found what he
was looking for all along:
a home and a family.

Paddington wrote to

his aunt Lucy in Peru.

He told her all about

his many adventures.

Paddington loved living with

the Browns

at Number 32 Windsor Gardens.

And the Browns loved
having Paddington
as part of their family.